THE ORPHAN GIRL'S WINTER SECRET

HISTORICAL VICTORIAN SAGA

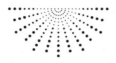

LILY FLETCHER
ROSIE SWAN

CONTENTS

CHAPTER ONE

At nine years old, Alexia Winters had just begun to realise that her family was poor. Not destitute, as her mother called the tragically thin women they saw sitting sometimes on the street, and not slum-dwellers, but poor. They lived in a little three room terraced house in the centre of Norwich, and although she rarely went hungry, food was rarely plentiful either. Although summers were comfortable, winters saw the family sleeping by the embers of the single fire, wrapped in as many blankets as they could muster.

But Alexia was rich in other ways. She had a loving mother and father who showered her with affection, and she had an inventive mind. She was always able to come up with a game or a story to play, using whatever props and playmates were available to her.

She was known to be something of a bossy girl, and her mother despaired at her ever growing into a more ladylike disposition. Although her father was stern with her when she misbehaved, he was secretly pleased to have such a bold and fearless daughter.

One autumn night, Alexia's father stayed up later than usual, as he was worrying about money. There was a certain irony in the need to light expensive candles to sit up, read the accounts, and worry about money, and Alexia's father was not unaware of it, but he felt that the expense of one candle would be worth it if he could only find the solution to his troubles. The weekly rent had gone up again recently, while Alexia's father's wages were the same. With the price of food rising too, he was concerned how they would make it through the winter. A loan, perhaps, would be the answer, although that brought many of its own risks. A new job, if he could find one, would help. Or perhaps the family would have to find cheaper accommodation, although he hated the idea of uprooting them.

Alexia's father puzzled over the problem late into the night, until his head nodded, and he fell asleep at the table, the candle still burning beside him. In his sleep, his arm knocked the candle to the ground, where it rolled, and the flame caught on the edge of the curtains.

Alexia's father slept on as the fire spread, unaware of the danger he was in. The smoke billowed around him, dulling his facilities, and by the time the fire spread to cover the wall, he was unconscious, unable to move or wake.

In the other room, Alexia woke up, blinking slowly at the burning sensation in her eyes. The air felt hot and heavy around her, and it tasted thick and poisonous. She had no light to see by, so for a moment, the darkness of the smoke seemed unremarkable. Then she heard a distant noise, a faint roar, and she sat up and looked around.

The door to the room was slightly ajar, and through it, through the thickness of the smoke, she could see a vague, flickering light. She blinked again, and then her young mind processed what she was seeing.

"Fire!" she shouted, and then immediately had a fit of coughing, the smoke rushing into her lungs. "Mamma, there's a fire!"

Her shout roused her mother, who leaped out of bed at once. The sound of the flames was growing louder, almost a roar. Alexia could not make out her mother's expression in the darkness, but she felt her hands fall on her shoulders, and the almost painful way she gripped them, reassuring her of her presence.

"Your papa," her mother said, through coughs. "Where is he?"

Alexia did not know. Alexia's mother strode toward the slightly open door, and then flinched back as the heat and smoke hit her.

"Not that way," she said. "Out the window, now, Alexia. Quick as you can."

Alexia's whole body was shaking, but she allowed her mother to haul her up onto the windowsill. "Papa!" she said.

"I'll get him," her mother said. "I'll be right behind you." She gave Alexia a little push, and Alexia stumbled through the open window. When she looked back, her mother had pressed the sleeve of her nightgown against her mouth and was running toward the living room, where her father must still sleep.

Alexia fell to the ground and stumbled a few feet away from the house. Around them, other households were waking, as the fire spread along the walls from home to home. Alexia was shaking from head to foot, and coughs wracked her whole body, the smoke still almost too thick to bear, but she dared not move farther away. Any moment now, her mamma and papa would follow her through the window, and they would all be safe.

She could hear screaming from the neighbours, but her own house was quiet except for the cracking of the walls and the roar of the flames. She stared at the window, willing her parents to appear.

They did not. Smoke billowed out of the open window, and a woman, a neighbour, eventually ran up and grabbed Alexia, hauling her farther away from the fire.

"No!" Alexia shouted, struggling with all her might. "Mamma!"

"It isn't safe, child," the neighbour said, but Alexia hauled herself free and ran. If her parents had not emerged through the window, they must have gone out through the front door. Yes, that made more sense. She would run around and see them standing on the street at the front, waiting for her.

She ran, but as she skidded around onto the street at the front of the houses, she heard a horrific crashing noise. The roof of her home was collapsing. Alexia screamed and ran even faster, looking desperately around the street for any sign of her parents, but there was none. They must have got out, she thought. They could not have been trapped.

More people were pouring out onto the streets now, and Alexia dodged between them, searching every face for her papa's familiar moustache or her mamma's smile.

Her parents were not there.

Eventually, men came in a great wagon to put out the fire. By morning, the street was smouldering, and Alexia sat hunched at a distance, watching, still waiting for her parents to emerge. She waited as policemen descended to investigate the scene, and as strangers began to search through the rubble, running away with whatever they could find. She waited as strange men began to clear the remnants of the house away, and the bodies of her mother and father finally emerged, limp and burned, and were put on the back of a carriage and carried away.

Alexia sat and stared, too shocked to cry. Her lungs still felt hot and raw, and her eyes were bleary. She rubbed at them with the back of one sooty hand, and when the pain in her stomach grew too much to ignore, she set off to try and find something to eat and drink.

Alexia's family had never been destitute, as her mother had called it, but Alexia had seen the poor children on the streets, the ones who did not have families and who her mama wished she could care for, but never had the money to spare for them. The boys, she knew, were half feral, running wild in gangs, picking pockets, stealing from bins, and charming people for a copper when they could. The girls were far sadder creatures. Alexia had seen them, dressed in ragged dresses, holding out flowers to passers-by and pleading with them to please buy one of the forlorn looking flowers in their hands.

As the days passed, and Alexia scrambled for food in bins, she began to realise that she was now one of these destitute children. She had no family other than her parents, and they were not coming back. No one would care for her now. She had to care for herself.

When she imagined that future, she knew she refused to be the waifish girl begging people to buy flowers outside the baker's shop. Alexia was a fighter, but no one would let her fight if they saw a shocked orphan girl in her nightgown, still sooty from the fire.

But no one would let her fight if they saw a shocked orphan girl in her nightgown, still sooty from the fire.

First, she stole a set of boy's clothes from a washing line, snatching them

and running as fast she could when no one was looking. Then she found a knife and sliced off her hair around her chin. Soon, she was not Alexia, but Alex, a wild thing, a survivor.

She missed her parents so much that it felt like a part of her had been physically wrenched from her chest, but Alexia tried her hardest not to think about that. Her priority now was to survive.

CHAPTER TWO

Casper Morton's gang of orphans and misfits was a regular sight around the back streets of Norwich. Made up of seven young boys in all, the gang would scurry from butcher to baker to grocer, inquiring after any odd jobs that might need completing for a little coin. Mostly, they acted as messengers and delivery boys, but they would take on any task that the proprietors required, whether moving heavy bags of flour or cleaning up blood.

Casper Morton was the oldest, and the clear ringleader of the group. He was fifteen, tall for his age, and strong, with a tangle of blond hair and the beginning wisps of a beard growing in on his face. He was also the most competent of the group, and the one you wanted for anything that involved particularly hard work, but the others listened to his directions, ran around on his behalf enquiring for work, and never seemed to argue back against him, as far as the adults around the city could see. Casper, for his part, was quiet in that confident, thoughtful manner that people might describe as 'stoic'. No one knew what led him to live on the streets from a young age, or why he decided to gather younger, less able, lads into his employ. The more mercenary in Norwich might assume he used the younger boys for his own gain, feeding them a little for their labour and then saving the money himself. Those who knew Casper better knew that was not true. Behind his quiet exterior, he was an optimist and an idealist. He dreamed of a better life for himself, one that could be reached through hard, honest work and determination, and he wanted to help the younger boys on the streets reach that life too. He remembered being ten and out in the cold, not knowing how to find food or warmth. He would not leave other boys to that fate if he could help it.

He currently had six younger boys in his gang. The next oldest, Timmy, was a black boy with a lot of spirit but not much upper body strength. His usual job was charming the shop owners into trusting the gang, wheedling any half-forgotten jobs out of the proprietor's memories, and winning them over so deeply that they felt compelled to enlist a bit of assistance in exchange for a little coin. David was the youngest, a boy of around eight, with prominent ears that stuck out perpendicular to his head. He was also the quietest, always quick to scurry to work but unable to answer even the simplest enquiry from a stranger with more than a squeak.

Casper's secret favourite was little Alex, a boy who claimed he was twelve but looked more like he was ten. They had found Alex three years back, and although Alex never spoke about what happened to his parents, Casper always imagined some disaster must have befallen them, like a building collapse or a fire, because Alex was always a little wary of sleeping inside walls. The gang slept in an old abandoned mining shed at night, and when Alex had first joined them, he screamed like he was being murdered at the thought of going indoors. Casper ended up sleeping outside the front door with him until slowly Alex built up the courage to sleep under the roof. Many boys would not have done the same, but it was a warm and dry autumn, and although Casper knew nothing about this new addition, he saw how small the boy was, and he knew that the streets would not be kind to him if he ran off and tried to survive alone.

Alex turned out to be more than worth the investment. He was a hard worker, always eager to pull his weight, and almost as good at charming people as Timmy was. Casper found himself frequently telling Alex to be quiet, for Alex loved to joke and chatter, and always had five opinions he wanted to voice when not even one was required, but despite his occasional sternness with the boy, Casper greatly enjoyed his presence. Alex was entertaining and a great asset to the group, and Casper was always intrigued by what outrageous things would come out of his mouth next.

Even on the rare occasions that Alex was quiet, Casper found himself watching him sometimes. Casper insisted, within himself, that he was just concerned about the younger boy's well-being, but there was something decidedly compelling about him, about the small features of his face and the confident gleam in his eyes.

Alexia,for of course that was who Alex really was, had not told a single soul about her past or her real identity since she watched her home burn to the ground. As far as her friends knew, she was an orphan boy, and she was happy to let them believe it. As Alex, she was strong and capable, able to pull her weight in the group. If they found out she was

Alexia, she did not know what they would do. They would kick her out, probably, and after losing her real family, she could not bear to also lose the new one she had found, just because she had not been born a boy.

Hiding the truth had not been difficult. The boys saw what they expected to see. They expected Alex to be a boy, so they never thought anything to the contrary. The only difficulty was when she needed to relieve herself, or on the rare occasions they all bathed, but the boys tended to jump into a trough of water fully clothed to wash when customers finally complained that they stank, and Alexia had managed to cultivate a reputation for herself as "shy Alex," always ready with a sassy word but strangely prudish when it came to getting undressed. No one ever suspected Alexia could be anyone other than who she claimed to be, so even if they found her behaviour odd, they never got close to considering the truth.

Alexia worried that her disguise would grow more difficult as she grew older, but far from shrinking into the shadows, Alexia reacted to that thought by being as outspoken and fearless as she could possibly be. The boldness already came naturally to her, far more than shyness did, and she often found herself talking back to Casper and arguing against his plans, even though she respected him deeply.

"I want to pair up with Timmy today," she said one morning, when Casper attempted to stick her with David. "We make a good pair. The baker on Elm Street likes us. He thinks we're funny! If we work together, we might be able to get some more coin."

"No joking around," Casper said harshly. "You'll earn more if you actually do the job they're asking you to do."

"They *like* it," Alexia said. "You're just jealous that they don't like you as much."

"Shut up, Alex," Casper snapped, and she flinched. "I've had enough of your nonsense. Do what you're told."

All Casper ever did was order Alexia around or shout at her, and Alexia was certain she heard harsh words from him far more often than the other boys did. The others could question him or joke around a little, as long as they did not take it too far, but any word that passed Alexia's lips seemed like an affront to the older boy.

"Why are you always the one in charge?" Alexia asked him. She could never resist talking back, no matter how much his reprimands stung. Negative attention from Casper always felt better than no attention at all.

"Because I am," Casper said. "If you don't like it, leave. Otherwise, get to work." Without another word, Casper marched away. Alexia watched him go, her hands tightening into fists. She felt tears burning in her eyes, but she refused to let them fall. She couldn't let the boys think she was weak.

More than anything, she wanted Casper's approval. She could never seem to earn it.

"It's alright," Timmy said to her, after Casper had gone. "We'll work together next time."

Alex just nodded and set out with David. He was a quiet kid, usually saying very little, but he had an expression of deep thought on his face as they walked, and eventually, Alexia couldn't stand it anymore. "Spit it out if you're going to say something," she said to him. "I can tell you want to."

David's ears turned pink. "Why do you and Casper always fight?" he asked.

"Because Casper is stupid," Alexia said, with more force than she actually felt.

"Casper's not stupid," David whispered.

"So I'm stupid?" she asked.

He shook his head. "You're not stupid neither," he said. "So why do you fight?"

The honest answer was that Alexia did not know. She cared deeply for Casper, and it broke her heart that he was far blunter towards her than to the others in the group. He was brave, she knew, and principled. He did not need to care for the younger boys as he did. He had not needed to take her under his wing and coax her into the group when she was alone and still traumatised by the fire. He chose to do these things, and that was admirable. It stung that he did not see her in the same positive light.

Recently, though, Alexia had begun to wonder whether thwarted admiration was all that fuelled the arguments between them. She found herself beginning to notice just how handsome Casper actually was, and sometimes before she fell asleep at night, she found herself thinking of his face, remembering a rare smile he had shared with one of the other kids, and desperately wishing the smile had been directed at her.

Casper would be disgusted with her if he discovered the nature of her feelings. He thought she was weak enough as it was.

The day, at least, turned out well. The baker's tasks were easy enough, and when he handed them coin for their work, he slipped them each an iced bun as well. Alexia and David sat in the alley behind the shop and savoured every bite, and for a while, she forgot her disagreement with Casper.

They did not mention the buns to Casper when they returned to the mining shed that evening, and Alexia thought perhaps getting paired up with David was worth it, because most of the others would not have been able to keep their mouths shut for even a moment. They handed their coins over to Casper, who counted them carefully and then divided up the meal for the evening in return.

"We got loads of money today," one of the lads, Johnny, said grumpily, as he picked at his slightly stale bread. "Why can't we spend it on anything *good* for once?"

Now Alexia was doubly glad they had not mentioned the iced buns. "We've got to save it," Casper said, with more patience than he usually would to a question like that. He must have been pleased with the day's haul as well.

"*Why?*"

"Our future isn't on the streets," he said. "One day, we'll make this a real business, and we'll have a real house too. But the only way we're going to do that is if we think now and save our money. It'll be worth it, in the end."

"I don't want a real house," Johnny griped. "I just want something good to eat. Like sausages! We could get sausages and maybe some bacon."

Alexia did not entirely disagree with him. Living in a house and having real jobs had not saved her mother and father in the end. In fact, she partly felt like the house was responsible for their deaths, the walls trapping them in with the flames when they would have survived beneath the open sky.

She was happy with her newfound family exactly as it was, with the mining shed and dips in water troughs and the delights of a surprise treat every now and again. The only thing she would change was the way Casper always seemed to be disappointed with her, but even that was at least familiar. She felt safe in this world.

That still could not stop her thinking about Casper's smile again as she went to sleep.

CHAPTER THREE

Alexia woke the next morning with terrible cramps wracking her stomach. She squeezed her eyes tight for the moment against the pain, wishing she could go back to sleep, but Casper was already shouting at the gang, hurrying them awake for the day's work. Alexia climbed to her feet, fighting back a moan. She would not give Casper another reason to be disappointed with her by complaining. All the boys suffered from coughs and colds and stomach complaints, thanks to the bad air and the chill and the filth in the streets, and Alexia refused to be one of the ones who used them as an excuse to lie in the shed all day instead of contributing. While Casper might have allowed little David to get away with that if he was unwell, she couldn't imagine him reacting with anything but annoyance and disdain if she begged off pulling her weight. Still, she struggled even to stand, the pain like a knife twisting in her belly. Perhaps she had eaten something bad, she thought, but everyone else seemed perfectly cheerful, and they all shared the same food. Alexia felt a jolt of fear that she might be sick, really sick, but she pushed the thought away. She couldn't afford to think like that. Still, she waited until half the boys had set out for the day, and Casper was directing the others, before sneaking out behind the shed alone. Her slowness earned her a rebuke from Casper, but she felt too tense to argue back.

Alexia tucked herself into a dark corner behind the mine shed and, making certain she was alone, pulled down her trousers to relieve herself. Then she froze. She was bleeding. Blood pooled between her legs, soaking into the dark cloth of her trousers. Alexia could not help it. She let out a loud scream, and she heard the voices inside the shed go quiet before footsteps ran towards her. She pulled her trousers up quickly, but her hands were shaking violently, and sobs burst out of her throat as she looked at the blood there again.

"Alex!" Casper crashed out of the mine shed, looking around for his charge. When he saw the shadow huddled in the corner, he ran forward, shouting. "What happened? Why're you screaming?"

Alexia couldn't speak. She just continued to sob, staring at the blood. She was dying, she thought. Her insides were falling out of her, and soon she would be dead and forgotten, like her ma and pa had been, like the bodies they passed sometimes on the street in winter, too cold to survive and with nowhere to go.

"You're bleeding," Casper said. He darted forward and grabbed her wrist. "What happened? Where're you hurt?"

Alexia continued to sob, too embarrassed and too afraid to speak. She gestured vaguely, and Casper considered her more carefully. When he spotted the subtle bloodstain he had missed before, he frowned in confusion for a moment, and then understanding dawned on his face.

"You're a girl," he said.

Alexia just shook her head, crying. She didn't know how he'd reached that conclusion, but now was not the time to give her secret away, not if she could avoid it.

She heard footsteps of a couple more of the boys emerge from the shed. "Alex's sick," Casper said loudly, without looking back at them. "Get to work, all of you. I'll handle it."

"Will he be alright?" one of the boys asked.

"He'll be fine," Casper said, and Alexia let out another sob. "Now get out of here."

With a little mumbling and several curious and concerned glances at Alexia, the rest of the boys departed.

"Why didn't you tell me you were a girl?" Casper asked, and although he did not dare to shout, his low voice conveyed his fury clearly enough. He seized Alexia's wrist. "Don't you know how dangerous that is? I've had you running around the streets for years, and you're a *girl*."

"I'm not," Alexia said, shaking her head furiously. She did not know what else to say. "I'm a boy!"

"Stop lying!" he said. His grip tightened on her wrist, and Alexia whimpered slightly. He immediately let go.

Casper ran his fingers through his hair, fighting to calm down. Terror seized his heart, making it impossible to think. Alex was a *girl*. If anyone else had found out… He swallowed hard. He could not bear to think of all that might have happened if she'd been discovered. The idea of any harm coming to Alex was more than he could stand.

"Tell me the truth," he said, finally, more calmly.

"What does it matter?" Alexia sobbed. "I'm dying."

"You're not dying," Casper said. Suddenly, he understood the scream and the sobs. "You don't know anything 'bout being a girl, now, do you?" he asked, his voice a little gentler. "How would you, I s'pose, running with us lot."

"I'm not" Alexia gasped, but Casper shook his head, cutting her off.

"I know you are," he said, "and if you had a mamma or a sister to teach you proper, instead of being stuck running with us lot, you'd know why. It's the woman's curse, Alex. That's why you're bleeding. It's--" Casper did not know how to explain this, especially to a sobbing girl he thought was a boy until two minutes ago. It seemed improper, somehow, to speak to her about it, but that was a useless thought. They'd run together for years, and she had no one else to speak to. He could maybe drag her to speak to the baker's wife. She was a kind lady, and she'd probably explain it to her, but then she'd know Alex's secret too. She might not be willing to let the boys do work for her husband anymore, once she knew Casper had risked a little girl like this. She might think he had been part of the deception, too.

It didn't matter, Casper decided, as Alex sobbed again. Alex was white as a fresh sheet, clutching her stomach, and Casper was not equipped to explain things to her properly.

"I promise," he said. "You're not dying. You're just getting a bit older. Come on. Come with me. We'll sort this out."

Alexia had no real choice but to sniff back her tears and follow him.

Casper was sitting on the step outside the back door of the baker's when Alex emerged, half an hour later, her face bright red but no more tears forming. The baker's wife put a bundle of rags into her hand and spoke a few words that Casper could not hear, her expression kind, and then she turned to Casper. She jerked her head, ordering him indoors.

"Wait here," Casper told Alex, and she nodded.

"You can't keep her running with you," the baker's wife said, as soon as the door was closed. "I can't allow it. It isn't safe."

"I know," Casper said. "I didn't know she was a girl until this morning. She hid it from me, too."

"The streets are no safe place for a girl," the baker's wife said. "Even less safe for a young lady like she's about to be. You understand me, boy?"

Casper nodded once, not speaking.

"You'll have to send her to the workhouse," the baker's wife said. "That'll keep her safe."

"Can't she work with you?" Casper asked, but one look at the baker's wife's face told him he'd more than pushed his luck.

"Here?" she said. "I have three little ones, and no room for any of them. I helped her just now, poor soul, because she has no mother or aunt or anybody to tell her the truth of things, and I'm glad you brought her to me. But I don't have the money or the room to raise a young lady like her and keep her safe, especially if she wants to run off with the boys, as I'm certain she's likely to do. I'm sorry, boy, but there's no help for it. The workhouse will be the safest place for her."

Casper nodded. "Well," he said. "Thanks for your help, anyway." He didn't really know what to say. Timmy was the eloquent one, not him, but Casper usually didn't feel quite so lost for words as he did now. Still, he nodded decisively, as though he had said his peace, and reopened the door to Alex waiting beyond.

CHAPTER FOUR

lex was sitting on the step outside, and Casper sat down next to her. "Alright," he said. "Talk. What's your real name?"

"Alexia," she said softly. "But ma and pa did call me Alex sometimes. That wasn't a lie."

"And how'd you end up here? Pretending to be a boy?"

"It's like you said," Alexia replied, some of her old defiance returning. "It isn't safe for a girl on the streets. I can't help being on the streets, but I could help being a girl, so that's what I did. Seemed better that way."

"Did you really think you'd get away with it forever?"

Alexia just shrugged. She had hoped that, at least. It had seemed far more possible before this morning began. Her stomach still ached fiercely, but she tried not to show it. She did not want Casper to think she was any weaker than she already felt.

"You know you can't stay with us now."

Alexia snapped around to look at him then, her expression fierce. "I can," she said. "As long as no one else knows, I can."

"I know," Casper said heavily. "And it's not safe."

"You don't have to tell anyone else," Alexia said. Her voice took on a pleading tone. "You don't. Just call me Alex and keep everything else the same. Please."

"I can't," he said. "It's not safe."

"I have nowhere else to go," she said. "What am I supposed to do, without you lot with me?"

"I'll take you to the workhouse," Casper said.

"No," Alexia said quickly. "Please. I won't. That's worse than out here!"

"It's safer," Casper said. "They have real places to sleep, to and work too. It's better that way, Alex."

She stood up, balling her hands into fists. "It's not fair," she said. "I'm as good as anyone in the gang. Why'd'ya always pick on *me*?"

"I don't," Casper said, bewildered.

"You do," Alexia shouted back. "You're always shouting. Nothing I do is good enough. Well, I s'pose you found your reason now, didn't you? Turns out I'm just a weak little *girl*."

"Alex." Casper grabbed her arm. "That's not true. I'm worried about you. That's all."

"Then let me stay," Alexia said. "I don't have anyone 'cept you lot. I don't have anyone else."

"You'll meet people in the workhouse," Casper said. "And we won't abandon you."

"You're abandoning me now," she said. She pulled her arm out of Casper's grip. "I won't go there. I won't."

"What happened," Casper asked gently, "that you ended up out here?"

Alexia scowled at him. She hadn't ever spoken about what befell her family, and Casper had hardly earned the right to hear the story now, speaking to her and threatening her as he was, but then she let out a breath. She could not convince him to let her stay if she refused to speak to him, and that was what she wanted more than anything.

"There was a fire," she murmured. "When I was nine. Whole house burned down while we were all sleeping. I woke up and everything was burning red and thick with smoke. I couldn't breathe. I tried shouting out for my ma and pa, but they didn't reply. And I couldn't see them. I couldn't see anything. I managed to climb out of the window. Whole place burned down. Ma and pa too. But I ran before anyone could catch me. I wasn't going to end up in one of *those* places. I could take care of myself."

"The streets are no life for anybody," Casper said. "'Specially not a girl."

"What difference does it make?" Alexia asked. "Whether I'm a boy or a girl, it's all the same. It's all as bad, ain't it?"

"That's why I want us to work hard," Casper said. "Eventually I'll get us all off the streets, you'll see."

"You're not sending the others to a workhouse," Alexia muttered.

"Listen." Casper put a hand on her shoulder. She scowled at him. "I'm not abandoning you, alright? I want you to be safe. But I'm gonna keep working with the others, and as soon as we get off the streets, we'll come get you. Alright? You won't be there forever, and we won't leave you. It's just a little while."

Alexia bit her lip.

"I promise, Alex," Casper said. "I swear on my life. It'll just be a little while, and you'll be safe. Then we'll get you out."

Alexia could no longer hide the fact that she was afraid. She had already lost everything she knew and loved once. If she went to the workhouse, she would be surrounded by strangers, forced to learn the rules of a new system alone, and the workhouse was a terrifying place. Everyone said so. She passed its stern brick walls sometimes. Something about that place screamed misery. From the way Casper was speaking, she was going to be alone again either way. He would not allow her to remain with the gang now. She could either go to the workhouse, with the hope, no, the promise, that Casper would eventually come for her again, or she could run away, never see her new family again, and start again alone.

"You promise?" she asked softly.

"I promise."

Alexia slowly nodded. Casper reached out and ruffled her hair, and she smiled, despite herself. "Come on, then," he said. "Let's get you sorted out."

The workhouse was as stern and unforgiving on the inside as it was on the outside. As soon as the wrinkled-faced old man inside realised that Alexia was a girl, only pretending to be a boy, he summoned a forbidding looking woman dressed in grey who all but dragged Alexia away. Alexia struggled against her, turning back to try and see Casper again, but the woman's grip was like iron, and she hauled Alexia into a narrow corridor and out of sight. At the last moment, she caught a glimpse of Casper handing a few coins over to the supervisor. The sight made her feel dirty, like she was being traded somehow, but even as she struggled, she knew that wasn't the case. Every coin they earned was precious. Casper must be trying to help her, in his own stupid way.

But Alexia did not feel at all like she was being helped. She had made a mistake in letting him bring her here. She would have been better out on the streets alone, she thought, as the woman roughly pulled off her boy's garb and scrubbed her down with soap and a brush. Alexia yelped in pain as the harsh movement scraped away her skin, but the woman did not slow down her ministrations. She was lecturing Alexia about proper decorum, about how she would need to behave like a chaste and obedient young lady here, and leave the rough habits and scum of the streets behind, but Alexia was not really listening to her, and all her words ran together. The woman forced Alexia into an itchy grey dress and cap and led her to a crowded dorm, full of other women and girls dressed in the exact same uniform. Very little light came in through the narrow dingy windows, and the air was heavy with the stench of work and despair.

Alexia was given a lumpy straw bed, crawling with lice, squeezed in against the wall. No one spoke to her. Everyone seemed too wrapped up in their own exhaustion and hopelessness to spare a few words for the new girl. She was put to work immediately, weaving together rope, and by the time the bell rang for supper, her fingers were rubbed raw from the coarseness of the task.

The evening meal, when they were shuffled to it together, was bread and gruel, and it left Alexia's stomach still growling with hunger. She ate it sitting at a long table on a long bench, under the watching eyes of another elderly-looking man wearing far finer clothes than anyone else was wearing.

Finally, Alexia was able to retire to her itchy bed to sleep, surrounded by the coughs and wheezes of dozens of strangers bedding down around her. The stern walls around her made her heart race, reminding her too much of the house she had shared with her mother and father, of the way the room had filled with smoke, and how the walls had charred beneath the flame. She pressed her head face-down into the pillow, ignoring the crawling lice, and allowed herself to give in to her anger again. She hated stupid Casper for forcing her here, and she hated her stupid female body for betraying her secret. If only Casper had let her stay with the gang, she wouldn't be here. If only she hadn't screamed when she'd seen the blood, she'd be in their old mining shed now, her true family around her. Through her anger, she could not deny that she missed him. She missed all of the gang, but she especially missed him.

Her fists clenched in anger, Alexia cried herself to sleep.

CHAPTER FIVE

The next few days in the workhouse passed in exhausting routine. The group awoke with the dawn, ate a thin breakfast, toiled all day, and then ate again before they were allowed to sleep. No one spoke to Alexia, and she spoke to no one. She missed her old gang so much that it was a physical ache, but the routine of the workhouse did not leave her much opportunity to think, and she was too tired after that first night to cry before she fell asleep.

Several days after her arrival in the workhouse, Alexia was alone in the washroom, after being ordered to leave her usual station to do laundry for her dorm instead. It was a small, cramped space, with barely enough room for the tub of water, the piles of clothes, and Alexia herself, but it was also one of the first times Alexia had managed to be alone since she came to the workhouse. As she scrubbed at the clothes, she heard the door open and then close behind her. Someone else had entered the room and was watching her.

She looked up and saw one of the supervisors, a heavy-set man who almost blocked the entire doorway just standing there. He looked down at Alexia with a slight smile on his face, and Alexia stood, her hands shaking. There was something in his expression that she did not like, a self-satisfaction and a belief in his own power that made Alexia want to run as fast as she could, but she had nowhere to go. The man was blocking the only door to the room.

She took a step backward, despite herself. "Can I help you?" she asked, sticking up her chin in defiance.

"You're new, ain't ya?" the supervisor asked. Alexia forced herself to nod, saying nothing. "What got you in here, eh? Hair short like a boy's. Not very respectful of a girl's place, now, is it?"

"I did what I had to," Alexia said. Her hands shook. "It's none of your business."

"Aye," the supervisor said. "I bet you did at that. Not bad looking, are ya, now you're all cleaned up. Even with that boyish hair."

It did not feel like a compliment. The man's leer made Alexia's skin crawl, and she took another step back, around the washtub, toward the window. She suddenly felt acutely aware of the threats that Casper had feared for her, out on the street, but the threat was not out there, with her found family, safe in the mining shed. It was here, watching her in the workhouse, intended to keep her safe.

"Don't come any closer!" Alexia said, her voice shaking.

"Or what?" the man asked, chuckling.

"Or I'll bite you!" she said defiantly.

The man laughed again. "'Course you will, sweetheart. That's why I gotta work to show you your place." With three long steps, he was upon her, his meaty hand gripping her arm. Alexia yelped and tried to struggle free, but his other hand came up and grabbed her under her chin. "Look at me, girl," he said, so Alexia did. She took in the delighted malice on his face and then she spit in his eye. When the man shouted in surprise, she kicked him hard on the shins, before wrapping her free hand into a fist and slamming it against the man's nose. The man was far bigger than she was, far stronger too, and could easily have overpowered her, but he seemed so startled by her attempt to fight back that for a moment he loosened his grip, and that was all that Alexia needed. She was used to scrapping on the streets, and she knew how to win a fight despite being small, underfed, and comparatively weedy. The trick was to move fast, to surprise your opponent, and then to retreat out of their range and reassess.

The supervisor still blocked the door with his body, so Alexia ran to the window. They were on the ground floor, thank Heavens, although there was still a good six-foot drop to the ground below, with bars across the gap. But there were only two bars, made to keep in people bigger and wider than Alexia, and she grabbed one with each hand, swinging her legs over the windowsill and squeezing her body through the gap. She jumped and released the bars, her hair and her dress flying up around her for a moment before she careened into the brick path below.

Her knee collided with the stone and pain burst all along her leg, but Alexia could not stop to consider it now. She took off at a run, hearing the supervisor shouting from the window above her, and dove into the cover of some bushes at the complex's edge. Once under their cover, she crawled on, trying to get as far away from the place where she entered as she could without leaving the greenery's protection.

Finally, she stopped and took a moment to catch her breath. Tears ran down her face. She missed Casper. She missed all the boys, but she missed Casper especially, no matter how angry and mean he had sometimes been. She wanted to sleep in that familiar mining shed, with her friends around her. She wanted her own clothes back, no matter how thin they had been, no matter how many holes she had had in her boots. But even if she left the workhouse now, she couldn't go back home. Casper wouldn't allow it. The only way she could be reunited with him was to stay here.

Here, where the supervisors cornered her when she was alone. Here, where she had now certainly made an enemy, a man with all the power to punish her for her rebellion. She had to go back, but her whole body shook with terror at the thought.

If anyone knew she had been out here, they would punish her for that too. No one would believe her story -- or if they did believe it, they would not care. Alexia furiously wiped the tears away from her eyes, struggling to catch her breath. She needed a plan.

She would wait until dark, she decided, and then sneak back in somehow. Perhaps she could climb in through the same window, with a little bit of effort and luck. As long as no one saw her coming back into the workhouse, she could sneak to bed and come up with some excuse to explain her absence in the morning.

She shivered and pulled herself into a ball against the cold. Her knee throbbed. But she was alright, she told herself. She was alright. She whispered the thought over and over to herself until exhaustion took over, and she fell into a restless sleep.

When Alexia woke up again, for a moment she did not know where she was. Twigs pressed into her cheek, and when she sat up, leaves rustled all around her. The world was dark now, and the air felt thick and heavy. She coughed as she rubbed her eyes, memories of events returning to her. Then she sat up straight. She had no idea how many hours had passes since she ran. It was clearly night, but she didn't know how late it was, or if her absence had been notied. Now that she was more awake, she could see light flickering too and wondered if they were searching for her.

She scrambled to the edge of the bushes, and then she stopped at the sight that awaited her. For a moment, she thought she was dreaming, trapped in her nightmares of that night three years ago, but this was real.

The women's dorm of the workhouse was on fire.

Smoke billowed out through the barred windows, and flames licked the roof. Alexia could make out figures at the windows, reaching out and shouting for help. Women were screaming. More footsteps pounded, and people poured out of the front doors of the workhouse, supervisors, men, children, but none of the faces Alexia recognised from her dorm.

Alexia stared at the flames. She could not look away. She heard the women's screams, and they rang like the screams of her ma, and her pa, as the fire overtook them. Alexia's whole body shook. She should help them. She should find a way to save the women screaming now, her dorm mates, to save them from the fire, but her limbs were frozen in place. She was trapped in memories of that night, the nightmare of it, the loss.

Alarm bells began to ring loudly, and more answered from the street beyond the workhouse. The fire service, she thought. They had done nothing to save her parents, but perhaps the workhouse had insurance, for the property if not for the people who lived within it. Running footsteps pounded the ground.

Inside the workhouse, something exploded. It was only a small explosion, just enough to hurt Alexia's ears and make the ground tremble, but it was enough to jolt Alexia out of her memories. She turned and ran. She could not have said where she was going, only that she had to *leave*, she had to put as much space between herself and the fire as she could. Her knee was still swollen and sore, and she stumbled once, her palms crashing against the pavement as she fell, but she barely paused for a second before she was scrambling up and running again.

She burst out of the workhouse walls and glanced back at the flames as she ran. She did not slow down as the ground beneath her shifted from pavement to road. She felt like the flames were lapping at her heels, and they would catch her and burn her if she paused, even for a moment. Then she heard a shout, and the panicked cry of a horse, right beside her. Something collided into her, and she knew no more.

CHAPTER SIX

"It's frightful," one woman said as she stood with her friend outside the butcher's. "All those people, trapped like that."

Her companion shuddered, but Casper stepped around the pair, paying little attention to what he considered to be rich women's concerns. The past few days had been particularly tough for him. The rest of the gang had been beyond upset when they'd learned that Casper sent Alex away, and became even more angry when they found out he'd led her to the workhouse. Casper tried to explain, as patiently as he could, that Alex was a *girl*, and that she needed to be safe, but the other boys would have none of it. Casper ended up shouting at all of them, telling them that *he* was in charge, *he* was the eldest, and *he* knew what was best for them all, and if they didn't like it, they could find someone else to help keep them alive. That had shut them up for a bit, but the boys were all still angry with him, and Casper had to admit that he was angry with himself.

He had had no choice, though. The workhouse was a terrible place, but at least it was safe. Anything could happen to a girl on the streets, and when he thought of someone hurting his Alex, the fear was beyond anything he could bear. Still, he thought about her constantly, and he missed her presence with an ache. She had always had a comment or a joke to make, and things were too quiet and dull without her. He resolved to work as hard as he could, and get the entire gang off the streets sooner, not later. The quicker they sorted themselves out, the quicker Alex could join them again.

That thought gave him purpose, at least, and allayed some of the guilt. But he still missed Alex and could not wait to be reunited with her again.

But when he entered the butcher's shop to enquire about any work for the day, the butcher had a grave expression on his face too. "It's a crying shame," he was saying to his wife. "They deserved more than that. If they hadn't been forced there in the first place--"

"It's that law," his wife said. "Forcing people into the workhouse just because they don't have enough to eat. Locking 'em up and not taking care of 'em. Those deaths are on parliament's hands, and everyone knows it."

"What's happened?" Casper asked loudly. Normally, he'd never interrupt a potential customer's conversation, as it didn't matter to him what they worried about, but the mention of the workhouse put him on edge. It sounded as if someone had died there.

"There's been a fire," the butcher's wife said. "All of Norwich is talking about it. They say it caught in the women's dormitory, and many of them were unable to get out. They locked them in at night to sleep, you see, so once the fire started and they tried the door--"

Casper did not wait to hear the rest. He was already running, out of the butcher's shop and down the road in the direction of the workhouse. All he could think about was Alex. Alex, who would have been sleeping in the women's dormitory. Alex, who had already lost her parents in a fire.

As he ran, he began to smell the lingering smoke in the air. It must have been a huge fire, then. And the butcher's wife had said there were *deaths*.

The workhouse was still smouldering when Casper arrived. Half of the building was blackened and charred, smoke still drifting lazily up from the ruins.A few people hung around the courtyard. "Alex!" Casper shouted, looking desperately left and right, frantic to find her face. "Alex!" He ran toward the building, and a hand rested on his shoulder, holding him back.

"No going in there, young man," a policeman said firmly. "It isn't safe."

"My friend was in there," Casper said. "Alexia. Alexia Winters. Where are the people who survived?"

"In the women's dorm?" the policeman asked, and Casper nodded. "I'm sorry, son, but almost all of the women in the dorm were killed by the flames. Twenty of 'em all told, bodies burned beyond recognition."

"Did no one get out?" Casper asked.

"A couple," the policeman said. "Badly burned too. Seems unlikely any of them will make it."

"Where are they?" Casper asked. The policeman nodded to another building across the courtyard, separate from the one that had burned. The workhouse infirmary must have been housed there. Casper barely paused to nod his thanks to the policeman before he was running again, crashing across the courtyard and pushing open the infirmary door.

The sight that greeted Casper would haunt him for the rest of his life. The air was rancid with the smell of burned flesh. Several figures lay in beds, uncovered by clothes, their blackened, peeling skin open to the air. Some were moaning softly. Others made no sound at all, gave no sign that they even still lived. Casper had to fight back the urge to vomit at the sight. He pressed a hand over his mouth and forced himself to step farther into the room, taking in everybody on every bed. He did not know which would be worse, finding Alex here, in pain, or not finding her at all, knowing she most likely was already dead.

None of these women could have been his friend. Most of them were too tall, too old. The one body that might have been Alex had wisps of long blonde hair, completely different from Alex's short brown mop. Still, she had to be somewhere. She *had* to be.

He turned to the woman who seemed to be on duty. "Alexia Winters," he said. "Is she here?"

"Can't you see I'm busy?" the woman said to him, without looking up. "We haven't had a chance to ask any of their names. They can barely stay awake as it is, and lucky for them at that."

Casper hurried after her. "But did any of the women escape?" he asked.

"They were locked in," the nurse said. "They're all either here or out back to be buried." The woman said something else afterwards, but Casper did not hear her. Blood rushed in his ears, drowning out all other sound. Alex was not here, which meant that she was out *there*. The fire had got her.

Alex had been locked in a burning building, all because of him. He had been the one who insisted she go to the workhouse. He had been the one to insist that she would be safe there.

Casper stumbled out of the infirmary and walked around the back, to where bodies had been laid out. All of them were charred and distorted beyond recognition. He could not possibly have picked out Alex's face from among them, but several of the bodies looked around the right size. There could be no mistaking what happened to her, no room for realistic hope. Alex was dead, and Casper had helped kill her. He stumbled as he walked, catching himself against the infirmary wall. That smiling, gutsy face, burned beyond recognition and lost forever. No matter how hard he worked, Alex would not be coming back.

Tears burned in Casper's eyes, blurring his vision. He wiped them away with the back of his hand, but more followed them. He was shaking. He felt as though he might vomit.

His Alex was dead, and nothing would ever bring her back.

Meanwhile, across the city, a rich man and his wife tended to an unconscious girl who had run out into the street and been struck by their hurrying carriage. Her entire left side was covered with bruises, and she had yet to awaken from the ordeal. The doctor said she was likely to survive, but they could not assess the damage done to her until she awoke. The woman dabbed at the broken girl's forehead with a damp cloth, murmuring comforting words to her, wondering what could have happened to this girl with hair like a boy's, and who she could possibly be.

CHAPTER SEVEN

Four Years Later

Casper Morton took his usual route to the cemetery, a bunch of carnations in his hand. When he had first begun to visit the unnamed graves of the women who died in the workhouse fire, he had been forced to collect whatever wildflowers he could, unable to afford anything more formal, but the past four years had been good to Casper, at least as far as business went, and now he could afford a small bunch of carnations every week to place on the grave. He could not have named a single flower when he first visited the flower seller, looking for something to buy, but the carnations had struck him with their vibrancy, and he had known immediately that they were the ones that suited Alex the most.

Not that there was any confirmation that Alex had been among the dead of the fire. No one had ever identified the bodies. But if Alex, or Alexia, as he tried to think of her, had survived, she would have appeared in the four years since that night. She would not have allowed everyone to believe she was dead, no matter how angry she had been at Casper for sending her away.

Now nineteen, Casper had grown taller and broader since the day he last saw Alexia, his blond hair complemented by darker blond stubble on his chin. He looked like a man now, and one who was accustomed to hard work, with muscles built over years of carrying heavy sacks and crates, and skin that was well-tanned by the sun. The loss of Alexia had only given him more drive to improve the gang's lot, and soon after her death, he invested all the group's coin into purchasing a cart to allow them to take on more intensive jobs for the businesses around Norwich. Some of the boys had balked at this expense and the extra work of dragging a handcart around, for they could not afford anything like a horse, but Timmy and David had stuck with him, and so had the stubborn but hard working thirteen-year-old, Christopher.

The cart had also brought in other money so that they had soon been able to purchase a second one, and then a third. Now the gang had a real street cart, pulled by an old mule they had been able to bargain at a great discount due to its damaged leg. The boys had taken careful care of the mule, who they called Ed, and although he still walked with a bit of a limp, and was slower than most owners would probably prefer, he got them and their cargo where they needed to go, and the boys were becoming almost respectable in their reputation around the city. Casper rented a house that was only in the third worst part of Norwich, and he had hopes of being able to upgrade to the *fourth* worst region soon. The other boys lived with him, as his employees and his friends, all agreeing it was better to save money that way.

No matter how hard Casper worked, his life felt incomplete. He had never been able to forgive himself for Alexia's death, and no matter how hard he worked, all he could think was that she should have been there to share in the rewards. He lay the fresh flowers on the grave shared by all the women killed in the fire, twenty-six in all, and gave the plot a respectful nod before stuffing his hands into his pockets and striding away. He wished he could do more, but there was always more work to be done to improve the boys' lot.

Meanwhile, a hundred miles away, a nameless orphan girl toiled in a convent kitchen. The workhouse owner who had discovered her had called her Jane, and so that was how they all referred to her, even though all knew it was unlikely to really be her name. She had been knocked down by the workhouse owner and his wife's carriage while they had been visiting the owner's elderly parents back in Norwich, and considering both her injuries and the disaster that had so recently struck at the city's workhouse, they felt obligated to care for her until she returned to health. They brought her back home to London with them, but when the girl finally awoke, it was with no memory of who she was or where she had come from. She had been wearing a workhouse uniform, so it did not seem likely that anyone was looking for her, or so the workhouse owner and his wife had supposed. They had named her Jane, and once her bruised and broken limbs had healed, the workhouse owner found her a place at the convent across the street from his own domain.

Jane was a quiet girl, always ready to follow orders, and rarely speaking a word. She walked with a slight limp from the accident, and she often seemed lost in her own thoughts. The nuns assumed she was about sixteen now, almost old enough to say her vows, and they had all abandoned trying to ask her about her past. The girl remembered nothing, and likely never would.

They could tell that Jane had been poor and uneducated, because she was terribly skinny, and she did not know how to read. The nuns, with so many under their care, were able to extend only limited affection towards her, or any of their charges, but illiteracy was something they felt compelled to address. Despite being so old to begin, little Jane took to reading quickly, with a natural talent for understanding the heart of things. Soon, this girl with no past and no apparent future fell in love with stories, filling the gaps in her memory and her heart with tales from Shakespeare, Keats, and Spenser. She especially loved Shakespeare's more cheerful plays, where disaster struck but love and ingenuity won the day. Her favourite, of all the tales she read, was "The Merchant of Venice." She liked to think that one day, perhaps she would be bold and resourceful like its heroine, and not trapped in a workhouse or convent with no sense of who she was.

The girl known as Jane began to have nightmares that she did not understand. She awoke screaming in the night, her mind full of thick smoke and flickering flames. The nuns would reprimand her for making such a fuss if they heard her, so she quickly learned to stifle her own cries, but that did nothing to calm the terror that filled her every time these dreams appeared. Sometimes, she dreamed she was inside the burning building, scrambling away from the smoke and crying out for her parents. Other times, she dreamed she was outside, hearing others scream in agony as smoke billowed through barred windows.

Jane thought on these dreams as she worked, trying to figure out what they might mean, and she was corrected many times by the sisters for her distraction. Jane was certain these dreams must have something to do with her past and the memories she had lost, and although the truth must be terrifying, to have become lost in memories of flames, she desperately wanted to know who she was and where she had come from. She tried to ask the nuns again about where she had come from, but all they could tell her was that her benefactor had picked her up after an accident on the street, and that his benevolent generosity was the only reason she was alive. God had spared her, the nuns would always say, so she could best thankHim by being quiet and doing exactly as she was told.

The answer to her past, when it came, appeared to her in a dream. She dreamed she was sitting on a step in an alley behind a shop, with a tall, handsome boy beside her. *Casper*, her dream self-thought. His name was Casper. He was telling her that he was going to keep her safe. "Go to the workhouse," he told her, "and when I have a house, I'll come get you." Jane was panicking, shaking her head, but Casper put a comforting hand on her shoulder. "Alex," he said, and then, "Alexia. I will come back for you."

When the girl known as Jane awoke this time, she did so with a gasp, not a scream. *Alexia*. Her name was Alexia Winters. She was from Norwich, not London, and she had friends, once. She had a family that she made after her parents were lost. A boy had promised to return for her. They all seemed so far away now. She did not know how she had lost them, only that she had. Now that she remembered, she knew she had to find this boy, if he still lived. She had to find out who he was, and what he knew.

CHAPTER EIGHT

As soon as Alexia's memories trickled back, a glimpse here and a glimpse there, she began to plan her escape from the convent. Leaving and returning to Norwich was not as simple as wishing for it, though. High walls surrounded the convert, and the iron gates were kept locked unless visitors were coming or going. The sisters put their orphan wards to work, and they were deeply concerned for their safety outside the convent walls. They could not risk any of their charges deciding to escape.

Alexia revealed to no one what she had remembered. She continued to play the role of the shy, obedient orphan with no memory of her life before, and she listened and waited for opportunity to come. Now that the floodgates were open, she began to remember more and more about her past, about the parents she had lost, and the attack of the man at the workhouse and, most of all, of Casper. Casper's goodness, Casper's temper, Casper's smile. Casper promising that he would come back for her He hadn't found her in all the years she'd been gone, even though he had promised he would come for her. Perhaps he had forgotten about her.

She needed to know the truth. Even if Casper had abandoned her, she was not afraid. Now that she remembered who she had been and all she had gone through, she knew that she could survive the world outside the convent by using her wits. She just needed her chance.

One afternoon, about a month after her dream, Alexia saw her opportunity. She was scrubbing pots in the yard behind the kitchen, her fingers chapped and raw from the work, when a cart drove into the yard, loaded high with firewood. She watched out of the corner of her eye as the driver began to offload the delivery into a pile. Once the cart was empty, Alexia knew, he would refill it with the rubbish piled against the kitchen wall to haul it away.

Alexia eyed the rubbish carefully. There were several sacks, some full to bursting with garbage, some lying limp and empty. Alexia considered one. She was still small and skinny for her age, thinned out by years of hard work and little to eat. She was certain she could fit inside one of the burlap sacks if she curled into a ball. As long as no one saw her hiding, the man would throw her onto the cart, as he never seemed to pay much attention to his work, and she would be carried through the open gates without anyone knowing she was there.

She had only a moment to decide. One of the sisters stepped out of the kitchen and began to shout at the man, telling him to bring some of the firewood inside. The man seemed disgruntled by her orders, based on the expression on his face, but he seemed to decide that it was not worth arguing with a woman of God, because he simply nodded and pulled some firewood back onto his shoulders to carry after her.

As soon as the man stepped through the kitchen door, Alexia grabbed a peeling knife from near the door and ran. The rubbish stank, but Alexia had survived much worse. She imagined she had smelled much worse, sometimes, while living with Casper Morton and his gang. Without a moment of hesitation, she crawled into one of the sacks and curled up among the potato peelings and food remains to wait.

She did not have to wait long. A few minutes later, the man returned. She heard him muttering to himself as he hauled up the sacks around her and tossed them into the cart, and then he picked up Alexia's sack. She fought to keep herself as still as possible, her limbs tucked against her body so that their shape did not give her away.

"What're they throwing away?" the man muttered, as he hauled Alexia across the yard. "Bricks?" He threw Alexia onto the cart, and she landed with a thud. Her damaged knee cracked against the bottom of the cart, and she bit her lip to stop herself from crying out in pain. She felt a few more thuds around her as more sacks of rubbish were added to the cart, and one landed half on top of her, forcing the air out of her lungs. Alexia screwed up her face and her courage, refusing to move even an inch, and eventually the barrage stopped. She heard the man say a few distant, indistinct words, and then the carriage shifted with his weight as he climbed into the seat at the front. With a click of his tongue, he encouraged the horse forward, and it set off with a gentle, rocking pace. Alexia listened to the clip of its hooves on the stone as it pulled through the yard, towards the gates. It picked up pace, sending Alexia swaying gently one way and then the next, as it pulled onto the road and away from the convent.

The journey lasted at least an hour, but finally, the movement of the cart stopped. Alexia waited for the man to unload the rubbish, but all she heard was his footsteps fading away. She waited for another ten minutes or so, listening for any sign of witnesses, and when none came, she attempted to climb out of the sack. But the burlap had become twisted around her during her journey, and Alexia could not seem to extricate her limbs from it well enough to find the opening and climb free. After a few minutes of struggle, she pulled out the peeling knife she had grabbed for self-defence and sliced the side of the sack instead. A few moments later, she and the potato peelings were spilling out into the open air.

The world around her was dark. The cart had stopped on a country road, and a little way away, Alexia could see an old, slightly run-down house with candlelight in the window. The man must have retired for the night.

Alexia sat up straighter and looked about, wondering whether she should run. She had no idea where she was, and she could be miles from the next nearest house. Running through a strange landscape in the dark seemed unnecessarily risky, when no one was likely to find her here or even look for her until morning.

Instead, she pulled the remains of the sack over herself and grabbed a few other rags for protection against the cold of the night. She put together a feast for herself from the food scraps around her, and then she lay down to sleep, trying to pretend that she was not shivering.

As she tried to sleep, she turned her head to look up at the sky and the stars. She had not slept under them for years, and their gleam had become little more than a dim memory, but the sight of them made her smile now. They reminded her of nights lying outside the mining shed with Casper beside her, keeping her company when she screamed and refused to sleep inside its walls. She had changed her mind eventually, of course, with some coaxing from the others once the cold set in, but for all those weeks, Casper had never given up on her, making sure she felt safe.

She wondered where he was now. She wondered if he was still alive. Perhaps he thought that she was dead. If he did not, he would certainly think that she had run away and abandoned him. She wanted to find him. Even if he no longer wanted to see her, she wanted them both to know the truth.

With these thoughts and memories filling her head, Alexia fell asleep.

When she awoke, many hours later, it was to a loud shout. She sat up with a jerk, looking around panicked for the source of the noise. The cart owner was back, and he had discovered her.

"What d'ya think you're doing?" the man shouted at her. "Get out of here!"

Alexia almost apologised, but then she thought better of it. She scrambled out of the cart in the pre-dawn light, dragging bits of cloth and potato peelings with her.

"I ain't running a charity for the mad here!" the man said. "Go on, get out."

Alexia felt quite mad as she found her feet, covered in dirt and leftover food. Her brown hair was tangled around her face, and she could smell that bits of potato had gotten stuck in it. The man was looking at her with frustration and disgust, and Alexia could have laughed. He did not suspect her at all. He thought her a passing mad woman who had chosen to bed down in rubbish for a night. She let out a giggle, and the man looked even more alarmed at that, as though her madness might be contagious.

"Tell me which way to town!" she said, still laughing. The man frowned at her, and she laughed some more. "Come on, quickly. Which way?"

The man pointed vaguely ahead of him, and Alexia sank into a parody of a curtsey. "Thank you kindly, sir," she said. "May England smile on you for your kindness." And still laughing, certain that the man found her quite insane, she set off down the street.

CHAPTER NINE

Meanwhile, in Norwich, Casper's business continued going from strength to strength. Ed the mule was a powerful asset, and now that they no longer had to rely on the boys' carrying power, they could take on larger jobs and complete them even faster. Casper was always careful with the money they earned, investing what was necessary back into the business, spending as little as he could on rent, and saving the rest for whatever uncertain future awaited them. He and the boys were off the streets, but he still wanted more for them. A better house, in a better neighbourhood, perhaps. Maybe one day a house that was just his own, in case he ever wanted to take a wife and have a family of his own.

But whenever he thought that, he remembered Alexia, and marriage and happiness seemed impossible, hopeless. She had been the girl for him, he thought. She had been right there beside him, and he had pushed her away. Her death would never leave his conscience, and marrying another girl felt like it would be an insult to her memory, somehow.

Even if Casper was not interested in other girls, other girls were interested in him. Chief among his admirers was the butcher's eldest daughter, a kind-seeming girl of eighteen called Rebecca, and although he could not reciprocate her feelings, her kindness towards him warmed him. She was always sneaking him little gifts of meat when he arrived to work for her father, and she spent as much time as possible in his presence, asking him about his work and his family and the other boys.

There was no denying that she was a pretty girl, well fed with thick brown hair and a sweet, round face, but although Casper could recognise her merits on an objective level, her beauty did not move him. Casper's heart was still buried in the cemetery with Alexia, wrapped up in his feelings of guilt and loss. He was not interested in marrying, or even in casual flirtation. His priority, his *duty*, was his business and the protection of the boys that followed him.

Still, Rebecca would try and tempt him to spend more time at the butcher's, coming up with excuses to delay his departure and inviting him back for reasons that got flimsier and flimsier every time. Once, she kissed him on the cheek as he departed, and Casper felt himself blushing.

"She's a bright young girl," the butcher mentioned to him casually once, when Rebecca was out of earshot. "And you're a solid young man. I wouldn't oppose it."

Casper wanted to tell him that he was not interested in marriage, but he rarely spoke to any of his clients, even when spoken to, so he remained silent, allowing the butcher to think what he would. After that, Rebecca's invitations became more frequent and more obvious, and although Casper politely refused her every time, she was undeterred.

Casper began to think that he may be forced to speak more bluntly with her, tell her at least something of Alexia and how he never planned to marry, but the conversation felt terribly uncomfortable, and he did not know how to begin. If he spoke up, he would hurt Rebecca's feelings and certainly provoke her anger for his presumption. Perhaps it was presumptuous of him. She had not told him that she cared for him yet. He could have been imagining the entire thing.

Casper was sitting in the downstairs room of the gang's shared house one Friday night, looking over their finances while the other boys slept. It was a dark, moonless night, the streetlamps had been lit hours before, and even the traffic of passing carriages had quieted to a trickle as the night grew late. The fire had mostly burned down, but Casper did not see the need to add more fuel when he had an oil lamp to see by and would be retiring himself before too much more time had passed. He wanted to save every penny he could.

Someone rapped on the front door. Casper paused mid-calculation to look. He wondered who would be calling at this hour. Perhaps one of the boys had snuck out was had been unable to sneak back in. He fought back a smile as he imagined David standing sheepishly in the doorway, forced to admit his rebellion to escape sleeping out in the cold. He peered through the window at the path before their house, half-expecting to see David's red face staring back at him, but then he saw that the visitor was a woman. He could see her skirts brushing against the ground, but the world outside was dark, and he could not make out her face beneath her hood.

Casper hurried to the front door. A woman knocking on his door this late in the evening might be in trouble, in need of help. The streets of Norwich were not as dangerous as they had once been, but scoundrels and villains could be found everywhere. A woman must be truly desperate if she needed to plead assistance from a stranger at this time of night. He pulled open the door with a little too much force, and the visitor on the doorstep flinched back.

"I'm sorry," he said quickly. "How can I help you, ma'am?"

The visitor pulled back her hood, revealing her face, and Casper was surprised to realise that she was not a stranger at all.

It was Rebecca.

"Rebecca," he said. "What's the matter?"

"May I come in?" she asked softly. Casper nodded and stepped aside for her to enter.

"What's happened?" Casper asked. "Why aren't you home?"

"Nothing's happened," Rebecca said, with a smile. "I was just out for an evening walk, and I wanted to see you." She walked past him, into the room that the boys used as their living room and kitchen. Casper followed her, feeling nonplussed.

"You wanted to see me?" he repeated. "How'd you know where I live?"

"Oh, my father knows, of course," Rebecca said. "He has it noted down with all his business things. It didn't take long to find it."

Casper paused in the doorway, watching Rebecca as she looked around the room, taking in the threadbare furniture and the unwashed dishes abandoned on the table. She wrinkled her nose slightly as she turned back

"Why were you looking for it?" Casper asked. Something felt wrong here, although he could not have said what or why. Rebecca was a nice enough girl, and she was no threat at all, but the hairs on the back of Casper's neck stood on end, telling him to be on his guard.

"Because I wanted to," Rebecca said simply. "I wanted to be able to see you. You never stay for long when you come to my father's shop."

"I have a lot of work to get to," Casper said.

"Yes, you're very hard working," Rebecca said, and Casper could not quite tell whether she was mocking him or not. "But you're not working now, are you? So, I thought I would see you."

"Rebecca," Casper said, stepping into the room now. "Your ma and pa'll be worried about you if you don't head home quick. It's not safe out at night."

"Oh, I'm perfectly safe," Rebecca said. "I'm with you, aren't I?" She moved back towards Casper and took his hand, lifting it between them. She squeezed, once. "Don't you want to see me, Casper? We never get enough time to talk."

"I do like talking to you, miss," Casper said. "And I do like seeing you. But now isn't the best time."

"Now is the perfect time," Rebecca said. She tugged on his hand, pulling him closer. "We're alone, aren't we? No one to disturb us. And I've been thinking of you." Her voice got lower, quieter. "I think about you all the time." She tugged him closer still and rose up on her tiptoes to press her lips to his.

Casper stepped back at once, pulling his hand free. "Maybe you should be going," he said.

"I don't want to," Rebecca said. She followed him, this time putting a hand on his shoulder. "We never get time to be alone." She leaned in again, and Casper scrambled away, back toward the door.

"I'm sorry," he said, "if I've given you the wrong impression. You're a nice girl, Rebecca. But I'm not--

I don't plan to get married. I gotta look after the boys."

Rebecca laughed. "Who said anything about getting married?" she asked. "I don't want to marry you either right now. I just wanted us to get to know each other better."

"Rebecca," he said, more firmly this time. "I don't think that's a good idea."

"Well, *I* do," Rebecca said. "Why, you got another girl? I've never seen her."

"No," Casper said. "I just don't think it's proper."

Rebecca laughed again. "Proper?" she repeated. "I should be the one worrying about what's *proper*."

"Yes," Casper said harshly, "you should be."

Rebecca's smile vanished. "Why are you being like this?" she asked. "I'm a better girl than you could ever hope to get."

"That's not true, miss," Casper said. "I've known better. I'd appreciate it if you saw yourself out."

Anger clouded Rebecca's face. She stared back at Casper for a moment, and then her lip trembled, and she burst into tears. Casper stood back, impassive, as she sobbed. It hurt his heart to see her hurting like that, but he could not see how he could comfort her without giving her the wrong idea about his intentions, and he would not behave in a dishonourable manner towards her, not for anything. His principles were as important to him as the young lady's wellbeing, and both would be compromised forever if he gave into her demands.

Rebecca pressed a hand to her mouth and continued to sob, but Casper said nothing more. Giving a few more sobs, Rebecca pushed past him, heading for the front door again. As she reached the entrance, she turned back, her eyes meeting Casper's, full of anger and dejection. "You'll regret this, Casper Morton," she said, in a voice that was far steelier than her tears would have led him to expect. "I promise you, you willWith one last furious look at him, she fled into the night.

CHAPTER TEN

Casper was nervous to return to the butcher's shop the following morning, but work was work, and he could not fail to appear, or he would risk his whole business reputation. To Casper's horror, the butcher and his wife were both absent, on errands, and Rebecca was behind the counter, taking orders and collecting payments. When Casper entered, a couple of customers were talking to her, but they soon departed, with a polite nod to Rebecca and another to Casper as they passed. The bell on the door rang as they closed it behind them.

"Got a delivery for your father," Casper said. It seemed best to stick to business. There was no point in embarrassing the poor girl any further. "No one answered when I went round the back."

"No, they wouldn't," Rebecca said. "I'm the only one here. I'll go unlock the door for you, and you can unload. Watch the front for a second for me?" He nodded that he would, and Rebecca disappeared. When she returned, she smiled at him, and Casper thought that perhaps the previous night had already been forgiven and forgotten, an embarrassing snag in their otherwise professional relationship. He worked with the other lads to unload the cart, and then came back around the front. The shop was empty this time. Rebecca leaned against the counter, idly playing with a strand of hair that had fallen loose from her bun. She straightened when she saw Casper, and when she handed him his coin, her hand brushed his, just a little. She gave him another shy smile as she bid him good day, and Casper left feeling unburdened by the events of the night before.

When someone knocked sharply on the door of his house that evening, he was first startled, and then concerned. He thought it might be Rebecca coming back to talk to him, either for an apology or another attempted tryst. He peered out of the grimy window at the front door and was startled to see that two constables waited there.

Goosebumps rose on Casper's arms and the back of his neck, and his heart kicked into overdrive. The police never meant anything good. Something terrible must have happened. He hurried to the door, reminding himself as he did so that all of his boys were safely sleeping upstairs. The bad news, whatever it was, could not concern them.

When Casper pulled open the front door, the nearest constable looked him up and down, sneering. "Casper Morton?" he asked, and Casper nodded. The constable sprung forward and grabbed Casper by the arm, hauling him outside. Casper shouted in surprise and struggled, but the other constable grabbed his other arm, and together they forced his hands behind his back and into handcuffs.

"What's going on?" Casper shouted. "I haven't done anything."

"Oh, that poor young lady's told us all about what you've done," the constable said, dragging Casper away from the house. Casper tried to struggle against him, and the policeman punched him in the face. Casper could feel his lip swelling immediately, and he spat out blood as he fought to catch his breath. The constables took the opportunity to throw Casper into the back of the horse-drawn wagon and slam the doors shut behind him.

Casper stared out of the barred window as the horses began to move and his house faded away. Just as they were about to turn the corner, he saw a face appear in the still-open doorway, as the youngest boy, David, looked out on the street to see what was going on.

Casper wished he knew what was going on, too. He had the feeling that he was in the deepest sort of trouble, but he had not done a single thing that he could think of to provoke it. He had always insisted on following the law, even when he and the boys were on the street. It was the honourable thing to do, after all, and criminals, he'd found, did not manage to elevate themselves and get off the streets for long, if they managed it at all.

When they reached the station, the constables pulled Casper out of the wagon and dragged him inside. "Please," Casper said, growing more desperate by the minute. "Just tell me what I'm supposed to have done."

"You know exactly what you did," one of the constables said. "That poor butcher's girl. Defiling her, after her family did so much for you."

"Defiling her?" Casper repeated. He felt lightheaded with panic now. "That's not what happened. I never--"

The constable hit him again, and Casper fell back, sagging in the stronger man's grip. They dragged him into a room, empty except for a table and a couple of chairs, and then left. A few moments later, the butcher entered, looking grave.

"Sir," Casper said. "Sir, the police are saying I hurt Rebecca. But I didn't do anything."

"I'd punch you, lad," the butcher said, "but I see these men have already done a fine job of it. How dare you mistreat my daughter so. Her heart is broken. She has been sobbing all day, and it took hours to get her to admit what had befallen her."

"I'm sorry," Casper said.

"So, you admit to it?"

Casper frowned. "I admit to rejecting her," he said. "I told her I had no intentions of getting married, and she took it badly."

"So, you defiled my daughter, and when she asked you simply to marry her and save her honour, you refused her. And now you mock her for the harm *you* have inflicted."

"No!" Casper shouted. "I didn't. I never touched Rebecca. She came to me."

"You, you worthless piece of scum, came into my shop this morning, on business for me, and found my daughter quite alone. I have already spoken to two witnesses who saw you enter the store and remain when they departed. You then took advantage of my absence and the lack of other witnesses and attacked my daughter, before completing your job and leaving her there broken."

"I did not," Casper said. "She's lying."

The butcher seemed to swell with anger. "You *dare* to call my daughter a liar, after what you've done?"

"I take no pleasure in it," Casper said. "But I must! She *is* lying. I barely spoke to your daughter this morning."

The butcher turned away, his face purple with rage, as though he could not even bear to look at Casper. "My Rebecca is a gentle lass," he said. "And a kind soul. And she cared for you, we both know that. A care you took advantage of. But she begged me to make you an offer, and thinking practically, I have little choice but to agree. You have ruined my daughter. If she is with child from this, what will become of her? The only remedy is for you to marry her at once."

"*Marry* her?" Casper repeated.

"Make right what you have done," the butcher said, "and you will go free. But if you will not do what you can now to make reparations for your crime, then I will be forced to let the law handle this. You will go to prison, lad, and if I can get you hung for this, I will."

"Sir," Casper said. "I did not lay a finger on your daughter. I swear I did not. But I won't marry her."

"If you are innocent and a good man, like you're trying to claim," the butcher said, "why would you refuse?"

"Because your daughter is attempting to manipulate me! She came to my house last night, sir, and propositioned me, and when I refused, she told me she'd make me regret it. I s'pose this is the regret she was talking about. But I won't marry a girl who would do such a thing and lie like this, not even to save my own skin."

"How dare you call her a liar," the butcher shouted, spittle flying from his lips, "after what you have done?"

"I take no pleasure in it, sir," Casper said. "But I must, if I'm to defend my own innocence. I've done nothing wrong, and your daughter is trying to punish me for that."

"You will not marry her?" the butcher asked. "Despite the generosity of the offer, despite the price of refusing?"

"I will not, sir," Casper said. His hands shook slightly, but his thoughts were steady and clear. He would not dishonour himself and his life because of a lie. He would adhere to truth, and hope that the truth would deliver him. Even if it didn't, his conscience would be clear.

"Then I'll see you hang, boy," the butcher said, and Casper knew that he meant every word.

CHAPTER ELEVEN

Days and weeks passed, and Alexia made her journey north towards Norwich. Disguising herself as a boy had worked well once before, so she sliced off her hair at the first opportunity, changed into some boy's clothes she managed to steal from a washing line, and adventured on as Alex again. By doing odd jobs on farms when she could get them and picking pockets when she couldn't, she kept herself fed enough, and when she finally arrived at her old home city, she felt strong, reinvigorated despite the weeks of travel. The physical weakness and mental shyness instilled by the workhouse and convent life were fading away.

Norwich was little changed from four years before. Alexia walked with purpose, taking in the sights of familiar shops on familiar streets, heading toward the old abandoned mine shed where they had once slept. She took care to avoid the street of the workhouse, afraid she would have to see a burned-out husk left over from the night of her escape.

When Alexia arrived at the old mining shed, the building was empty. There had always been signs of the boys' presence around while she lived there, even though they had few possessions. The ash from a fire here, a wooden spinning top propped beside some blankets over there. Now the mining shed was cold and bare, the corners decorated with cobwebs, as though no one had stepped foot inside for some time.

Alexia's mouth went dry with fear over what might have befallen the boys, but she tried to shake that thought away. Casper had always insisted that he was going to get the gang off the streets, and he had promised he would work even harder after he sent Alexia away. They must have moved to another, better home.

Alexia looked at the familiar walls, trying to decide what to do. The only possible solution that she could think of was to ask about Casper's whereabouts, and her best chance for that would be to ask the businesses that they used to do chores for, in case they knew where he had gone.

Alexia did not want to be recognised as Alex, the little orphan boy who used to run with Casper Morton, if she could help it. She needed time to assess the situation first. She reached into her stolen pack and changed back into women's clothes before fixing a hat on her head at such an angle that it looked like it might conceal a neat woman's hairstyle and not a ragged boy's cut. Using water in a trough to scrub any remaining dirt from her face and judging in her reflection that she would pass for a woman, if a poor and struggling one, she headed to one of the baker's shops that they used to help. She would not risk going to the shop where the baker's wife had helped her several years ago, but there were several they used to work for around the city, and Alexia hoped one of those would know Casper's whereabouts before she had to risk somewhere where she was more familiar.

She knocked at the back door of the baker's, and when an unfamiliar woman opened the door, she bobbed into a curtsey. "Sorry to bother you, miss," she said. "But I know Casper Morton and his boys used to do some work for you. I was wondering if they still do? I need to find them. Mr Morton in particular."

The baker's wife clicked her tongue in disapproval. "The lads have already been round today," she said. "Might be back tomorrow, might be the day after. But if it's that Casper Morton you're after, I'd tell you to stay well away from him. Bad business, that."

"Why?" Alexia asked. Her heart started to pound faster. "What happened?"

"Attacked that sweet young girl, didn't he?" the baker's wife said. "It were in the papers, you know. He's locked up now, and I don't think he'll be coming back anytime soon, not in this life. The girl's father is determined to see him suffer, and who can blame him for that? No, miss, if it's hardworking lads you're needing, his boys are still as good as any, but I'd forget about that Casper Morton. He ain't a safe thought for a young thing like you."

Alexia forced herself to bob into a respectful curtsey and murmur her thanks. But inside, her mind was racing. Alexia could not believe that Casper had been arrested for attacking a girl. She would not believe it. Casper had always done so much to protect her. He had been wracked with guilt at just the idea that any harm could have befallen Alexia, after he found out that she was a girl He could not have attacked someone the way the baker's wife had said.

Alexia hurried away in search of a paper to read the charges herself, and they were exactly as the baker's wife had claimed. But Alexia still could not believe it. If Casper had truly grown into someone that cruel in the years since she had met him, Alexia would need to see it for herself.

Luckily, she was not too late for the trial. The newspaper stated that the court case would begin the following day, and Alexia spent a restless night in the abandoned mining shed, unable to rest until she knew the truth.

The next day dawned crisp and cold, and Alexia donned her boy's garb again before hurrying to the courthouse. The viewing gallery was almost empty, but she could see Casper standing in the box for the accused, looking down at his clasped hands. He had grown in the years since she last saw him. His shoulders had filled out and he had stubble across his chin, but Alexia still recognised him, and her heart fluttered at the sight. He was still the same old Casper, standing quietly, saying nothing, but with an aura of utter self confidence that Alexia could not mistake. He stood like a man who believed in his innocence.

Alexia slipped onto one of the viewing benches. Casper did not look up at her or seem to notice her arrival at all, and she was glad of it. As much as she wanted to see him, she did not think she was ready for any sort of reunion, not until she found out the truth.

She pressed her stubby fingernails into her palms as the judge read out the charges. He was a stern, heavy-set man, his wig ever so slightly askew on his head, and Alexia rather got the sense that he had decided against Casper, even before a single piece of evidence had been read. He did not even look like he was paying attention to events. He had cold sweat on his brow, and his eyes were slightly glazed, as though his thoughts were somewhere else. Alexia wanted to stand up and demand to know what was going on, the *truth*, but she knew she could not interfere. So, she sat, and listened, as the trial got underway.

The charges sounded so much worse when spoken aloud by the sombre judge. The few people in the viewing gallery murmured when they were read, despite the fact that most must already know them, and even Alexia felt her stomach twist in horror and disgust at the idea of Casper cornering a young girl in that way. If the charges were true, he was not the boy she had always believed him to be.

Alexia wanted the trial to hurry up, so that she could hear Casper speak in his own defence. But the judge was speaking slowly, his voice ringing through the courthouse in sonorous tones, and it took half an hour simply to confirm Casper's identity and all of the charges. The judge dabbed his forehead with a handkerchief several times, and occasionally he turned and murmured something to the clerk standing behind him. Something was wrong, Alexia thought.

Yet the trial continued at its snails' pace, and Casper had his chance to declare his innocence. He did not present an argument in his defence, however. He simply stated his stance, not guilty, and looked soberly back at the judge as though daring him to contradict him.

The judge dabbed at the sweat on his forehead again. He stood suddenly, and the entire courtroom gasped as he swayed on his feet, gripping the desk in front of him to prevent himself from falling over.

Then the judge fainted, and the entire courtroom descended into chaos. While the clerk fanned the unconscious judge, another official strode forward and declared that the trial would be adjourned for several days, and the few people in the gallery were quickly ushered out of the room.

It was bad luck on the judge's part, but not, Alexia thought, necessarily bad luck for her or for Casper. Alexia did not know whether Casper was innocent or guilty, but she wanted time to find this Rebecca, Casper's accuser, and see her for herself.

CHAPTER TWELVE

It did not take long for Alexia to find the butcher's daughter, and she watched her carefully from a distance as the girl dallied in the shop, serving customers. She was pretty, Alexia supposed, with thick brown hair and a kind smile, and she seemed genuine enough with the customers she spoke to. Alexia desperately hoped that Casper had not hurt her, as the charges stated. She could not imagine Casper being violent toward her, but she also did not look like a liar, and *why* would she lie about it, Alexia thought to herself. "Why on earth would she claim such a thing and compromise her own reputation and honour, unless it were true?" At the very least, Casper must have had relations with this girl, and even that thought made Alexia frown.

The Casper she knew would care too much about a girl's reputation to risk tarnishing it for his own pleasure, no matter how much he liked her.

None of it made sense.

Alexia needed more information. She watched Rebecca for the rest of the day, and then determined to follow her, as much as she could, to see who she might speak to and where she might go. Rebecca did nothing suspicious that first night, so Alexia followed her the next day and night too, as she worked at the butcher's, as she ran errands for her father, as she browsed other shops and purchased a pretty new ribbon and a few replacement buttons for a coat. She seemed utterly oblivious to Alexia's presence, and Alexia was starting to doubt that she would find anything useful before the next trial date, when Rebecca paused outside a fairly well-to-do looking house that was definitely not her own. At first, Alexia assumed she was paying a visit to a friend, but then Rebecca looked around, as though checking no one she knew was in sight, before hurrying to the door. She knocked on it three times quickly.

A man opened the door. He looked to be in his twenties, with neat blond hair and a suit that suggested he was a man of decent means, and it took Alexia a moment to recognise him. He was the clerk at the trial, the man who had tried to revive the judge after he had taken ill.

Rebecca shoved straight past the man into the house, and the man shut the door behind her.

Alexia scrambled forward, into the flower bushes beneath the window. If Rebecca was visiting a man from the court, it had to be related to Casper's case. She held her breath and listened.

"You shouldn't be here," the man was saying. "I told you that you needed to stay away 'til the trial is over."

"I needed to see you," Rebecca said. "I'm scared, John. Casper isn't giving in."

"He's a fool if he doesn't," the man said.

"Well, then he's a fool, isn't he?" Rebecca snapped. "Just like me."

"Come, now, Rebecca," the man said, and his voice somehow managed to be both gentle and mocking at the same time. "Don't be like that."

"Like what?" she asked. "Worried for myself? He's refusing to marry me, John. I'll start showing any day now, and what will become of me then, if Casper refuses to help me?"

"I don't know," John said, "nor do I particularly care. They'll still think the baby is his, won't they?"

"They might," Rebecca said. "But what will *I* do? I'm alone, John. I'll be ruined, even more than I am now. You are going to have to marry me. It's *your* baby, and it's your responsibility. I should never have agreed to this scheme in the first place."

Alexia struggled to stop herself from gasping. Here, then, was the reason. Rebecca was pregnant, but Casper was not the child's father. This scoundrel had forsaken her, and Rebecca had targeted Casper in his place.

The man merely laughed at Rebecca's outburst. "I've got no interest in marrying you, girl," he said. "You're a worthless woman without a shred of dignity. I don't want you for a wife."

"That's not what you claimed before," Rebecca said, and Alexia could hear the tears in her voice. "You told me that you loved me."

"Feelings change, Rebecca. If you want to get married, this fool of yours is your only hope."

"You'll pay for this," Rebecca said, through tears. "I promise you will."

The man laughed again. "Do your worst, girl," he said. "I look forward to seeing it."

CHAPTER THIRTEEN

B y the time the following morning dawned, Alexia had a plan to see Casper. She managed to steal a nun's habit that had been sent out for laundering, and four years living in a convent meant she could easily imitate a nun's walk and manner well enough to pass for one herself. She marked her face to obscure her features as much as she could, and the result left her looking somewhat scarred and pitiful. That was all for the better, Alexia thought. Armed with the knowledge she had gleaned from Rebecca, she headed to the city jail.

The constable who greeted her seemed flummoxed by her presence. His stumbling politeness suggested he was not entirely comfortable speaking with a woman of God, as though he thought Alexia might be able to read his sins and judge him on the Lord's behalf. He also seemed somewhat moved by her scars, and Alexia could see him silently inventing a new tragic past for this young, scarred nun, turning her from a creature to be scared of, to one of pity.

"I wish to speak to Casper Morton," she said, lowering her voice as much as she could to make herself sound older and more authoritative. "The Sisters of Immaculate Conception read about his case in the paper, and we are concerned for his immortal soul. If the man does not admit to his crime before God and man, then he cannot seek forgiveness, and we are committed to the salvation of all souls, no matter how tainted they may once have been. Please allow me to speak with him. I may be able to get him to confess."

"That seems unlikely, miss," the constable said. She let her disappointment spread across her face, and he added, "But I will not stand in your way if you wish to try."

Alexia soon found herself alone in a room with Casper. He stood a little awkwardly, waiting for her to speak, as though he too did not know quite how to behave in the presence of a woman of God. Alexia had thought perhaps he might have recognised her, despite her disguise, but he seemed oblivious, distracted by his own despair.

This suited Alexia's purpose well. As delighted as she was to see Casper alive and whole, she could not deny that it bothered her that Casper had sent her to the workhouse and then seemingly forgotten her. He had four years in which he could try to find her, and he had done nothing. There had to be a reason, and Alexia did not think she would uncover it if she addressed Casper as herself.

"I have come to you from the Convent of the Sisters of the Immaculate Conception," she told him, keeping her voice low again. "I have a message for you."

Casper looked mildly interested, but little more.

"Nearly five years ago, I tended to a girl who had been injured in a terrible accident on the road to London, outside the workhouse, and she has since become one of our wards. Her name is Alexia."

Casper gasped. He stared at Alexia for a long moment, seemingly unbelieving, then darted forward, as though he intended to grab her hands. He stopped himself at the last moment, but he continued to gape at Alexia like a fish.

"Alexia?" he asked. "I thought she was dead. I thought she died in the fire at the workhouse."

"She was near enough to dead when we found her," Alexia said, "and she lost her memory for many years. But it is beginning to return to her, and she remembered you."

"Is she alright?" Casper asked desperately, and he sounded so joyful and so panicked that Alexia almost broke down and told him the truth immediately. "Is she well? Is she--" He stopped himself, overwhelmed by the number of thoughts fighting for attention. "Tell me everything. Please."

"She is as well as could be hoped," Alexia said. Here, now, was her chance to test whether Casper was the man she had always thought him to be, a chance to find out his true feelings about her. "She was badly scarred by the accident, and her leg never healed right. She is a quiet girl, something of a recluse, and badly disfigured. But she began to recall a dear friend and protector called Casper Morton, and she begged someone to find him. We were horrified to find that name in the paper, and to discover what you had been accused of."

"It isn't true," Casper said. "I swear, it's not. I never did anything to that girl. She's framing me, blackmailing me, telling me I have to marry her, or her father will see me locked up or even hung. I refused to lie for her sake or to marry someone so manipulative, so here I am. Please believe me."

"I might be able to be convinced," Alexia said. "You speak like an honest soul. Alexia is still recovering her memory, however. Is there any message you might wish for me to bring her?"

"Yes," Casper said. "Yes, of course." He reached behind his neck and underneath his shirt, and he pulled out a locket on a long chain. He unclasped it and handed it to Alexia. "I bought this for Alexia," he said. "After I thought she died. There was a fire at the workhouse the night she disappeared, you see, and so many of the bodies were burned beyond recognition. I couldn't find her body, but I had no hope of her being alive, but I bought this locket to remember her by. I didn't want to forget her. When you return to her, give her this, and tell her-- tell her I care about her, and I always have. Tell her I'm sorry I didn't find her sooner. I visited her grave every week, and to imagine I could have been visiting her instead-." He shook his head, tears in his eyes. "It seems like it's too late for me to come for her now, but ask her if she has it in her heart to wait for me. I don't know how long I'll be locked up, or if I'll even get out of prison alive, but if I do- if I do, when I'm free, I'll come and get her. If she wants me to. I want to be with her."

Alexia felt tears forming in her own eyes, and she lowered her head slightly so that they were hidden in the shadow of her habit. She had not been mistaken. Casper did care for her. He had never abandoned his vow to return for her, and, more than that, he wanted to be with her. He remembered the scrappy little girl she had been, and he wanted the woman she had become in his life, no matter how disfigured she may be.

"Yes," Alexia said to Casper. "I will tell her."

CHAPTER FOURTEEN

Alexia returned to the mining shed, torn between triumph and despair. She had found Casper, her beloved, and he had not forgotten her, not even when he believed she was dead, but he was trapped in Rebecca's web of manipulation and lies now, and she might never actually get to be with him unless she could prove his innocence.

She put Casper's locket around her neck and looked down at the delicate silver design. The locket contained no picture nor lock of hair, for Casper had had neither when Alexia had left, but she could feel the love imbued in the metal, the way Casper must have held it and considered it and thought of her. She could not, *would* not, leave him to suffer.

She needed a way to present what she knew in court. Since she did not have any hard evidence, that meant she needed to get Rebecca to confess to the truth, in front of witnesses. Alexia did not believe that Rebecca would admit to it easily.

Her best chance, she thought, was to go to court disguised as a man, and somehow inform Casper's lawyer of what she knew. If the lawyer would not listen, perhaps she could speak to Rebecca herself, somehow convince her that she needed to speak the truth. It seemed like a weak plan, especially if the lawyer would not cooperate, but she had no other, and she was out of time. Casper's trial was starting again upon the morrow.

She took a seat as close to the front as possible and waited for proceedings to begin. This time, Rebecca was present to give her testimony, and Alexia saw her glancing at the clerk with whom she had met. She did not say a word to him. Alexia was trying to find Casper's lawyer, to speak to him about what she knew, but she could not find him. The prosecution spoke to Rebecca in a gentle, coaxing voice, and Rebecca tearfully recounted how Casper had worked for her father, and how he came to the butcher's shop one morning when she was working there alone. She sobbed delicately as she told how he had propositioned her, and how she had refused him, knowing it was improper, and not wishing to shame her family. She described Casper's anger in response, an anger that was so unlike Casper that Alexia was surprised anyone who knew him had believed it, and how he had attacked her. The judge nodded most sympathetically to her tale, while Casper just stared straight ahead, his expression unreadable.

Once the prosecution had finished their interview, another problem arose. The judge asked for Casper's counsel to speak, and Casper was forced to admit that his lawyer had not shown up at court. His voice shook slightly as he spoke, but he mostly sounded resigned. Alexia did not know how rich or poor Casper was, but she could not imagine that a lawyer would have come cheaply for him, and now it seemed that expense had been wasted. Casper must have paid the lawyer all that he could, but Alexia could easily imagine that another interested party could have paid him more to stay away.

Casper now had no lawyer, no advocate to speak for him, and no way to uncover Rebecca's lies. Alexia's hands shook at the injustice of it. She needed to do something to help him.

She was dressed as a man, and she had already come here resolved to speak on Casper's behalf. It would be just like the play she had read while at the convent, the Merchant of Venice. That had always been her favourite. She had loved how the resourceful Portia had dressed as a man in order to rescue Antonio from the greedy Shylock. Now it was her turn to put on a similar show.

She strode forward, putting as much confidence in her gait as she could. "I am from the office of Mr Morton's lawyer," she said, deepening her voice. "Mr Morton's lawyer is indisposed. I will be taking over his representation."

She half-expected someone to argue with her, but nobody seemed too interested in who represented Casper, as long as they could continue with the trial. Casper, however, looked astounded. He considered Alexia with narrowed eyes, as though trying to place her, and Alexia had to force herself to look away from him and look to the judge instead.

"Very well," the judge said. "You may proceed."

Alexia cleared her throat, steeling herself to speak. She had to be very careful with her words. She needed to guide Rebecca to a confession, without pressuring her so much that the court turned against Alexia for her seeming cruelty.

"That was a tragic tale," she said to Rebecca. "Most distressing to hear. But I wonder how it could have happened in your father's shop, as you suggest. Surely passers-by would have noticed your distress."

"He dragged me into the back room," Rebecca said. "He knew the place well, because he's done so much work for my father."

"I see," Alexia said. She had to go gently. "That must have been a frightful experience for you. I wonder, has it had any longer-term effects on your health?"

Rebecca paled slightly. "I don't sleep well now," she said. "And I'm scared to go out much."

"Your physical health," Alexia clarified. "It would be most upsetting to be in the family way after such an ordeal."

Rebecca blushed red. "If I were," she said, "it is not my doing."

"So, you believe you might be?" Alexia asked. "In the family way, I mean."

Rebecca could not meet Alexia's eyes. "I would not know," she said softly. "I am unmarried. I do not know much about babies."

"Surely you must know some of the signs," Alexia said. "You do not seem stupid nor naive. Can you say with confidence that you are not?" Rebecca said nothing. "Because I rather suspect that you are with child now, and that is part of your distress here today. Is that true?"

Tears burned in Rebecca's eyes. She bit her lip and nodded, and the courtroom let out a gentle gasp. "I suspect so," she said. "After what that villain has done to me, I was willing to marry him, if it meant some support and honour for my baby, but he refused even that."

"Yes, I see," Alexia said. She could feel the anger brewing in the courthouse around her, all of it directed at Casper for his supposed callousness. She had to tread carefully. "I imagine a young lady would be desperate for marriage, if she found herself in such a situation. Desperate enough to lie, even."

"I have not lied!" Rebecca said. "How else would this have happened? I tell you, he is a villain."

"I wonder," Alexia said, "whether that is the case. I wonder whether he violated you and you ended up with child, or whether you found yourself with child and so invented this story to cover your own tracks. Why else would you be so eager to marry a man you claim has hurt you in this way?"

"I don't have a choice!" Rebecca said.

"I believe you," Alexia said. "I believe you think you have no choice but to frame this man to cover for your own misdeeds." Rebecca shook her head fiercely. "This young man may hang for your lies. He will be locked up and his life will be destroyed, through no fault of his own. Can you live with yourself for doing that? Would you not prefer that the real villain be punished?" Alexia looked at the court clerk. "This man is the child's father, is he not? He is the villain who has abandoned you. But you would rather marry a good man like Mr Morton than a villain such as him, so you tried to frame him as the father, and when he refused your plan to seduce him, you forced his hand with this lie instead. But you have been thwarted, haven't you? He refuses to lie for you. He refuses to sacrifice his integrity, even if it means his own reputation, his own *life*. Are you truly willing to let this young man die to protect yourself? And to protect a man as cruel as this clerk, who has betrayed you?"

The clerk's face was turning purple, but Rebecca broke, her whole body wracked with her sobs. She was crying so hard that she could not speak, but she nodded her head through her tears.

"That's a lie!" the clerk declared, but then Rebecca shook her head, gathering her strength to speak.

"How did you know?" she asked Alexia in a whisper. "How did you figure it out?" Alexia said nothing, and Rebecca continued. "It's true," she said. "Casper never hurt me. I was just so desperate. John said such sweet words to me. He told me we would have a life together, and I believed him. But once I found out I was with child and asked him to marry me, he refused me. He laughed at me. I could not admit the truth to my father, and I knew the court would never convict one of their own. I had no reason to be alone with John either way. But I had always cared for Casper, and I thought that maybe I could persuade him. And when he refused, I couldn't not do it!" she added, sounding frantic. "It was him or me. I thought he would give in. I thought he would agree to marry me. I didn't think it would end up here like this." Her shoulders shook. "I'm sorry. I'm sorry."

"I rest my case," Alexia said.

For several minutes afterwards, the court dissolved into chaos and shouting. Eventually, the judge managed to bang his gavel loud enough to call things back to order, and he held people's attention long enough to officially throw out the case. He declared Casper a free man, just as Rebecca's father reached her, his face contorted with anger. Rebecca was still sobbing so hard that she had half-collapsed, and her father had to catch her to hold her up.

Casper watched Rebecca's tears with a look of concern on his face, and then he turned to Alexia. "Thank you, sir," he said. "You saved my skin. How did you know?"

"I did my research, Mr Morton," Alexia said.

"What happened to my other lawyer?" he asked. "I've never seen you before. How did you even know about my case?"

"My greatest concern is justice, boy," Alexia said, rather enjoying her role now that she was no longer afraid for his life. "And I have a message for you. But we cannot talk here. Perhaps somewhere more private?"

"I will follow you back to your offices," Casper said, but Alexia shook her head.

"More private than that," she said. "Perhaps your place of residence?"

"Oh," Casper said, looking surprised. "Certainly." He did not seem to understand why such a request would be necessary, but he looked unwilling to argue with the man who had just potentially saved his life. "I will lead the way."

CHAPTER FIFTEEN

Alexia struggled not to speak to Casper or take his hand as they walked through Norwich to his home. He was so close, and he was free. Alexia felt as though her whole future was now open to her, her misfortune at an end, and all she had to do was reach out and take it. But she felt suddenly shy. Casper might not really still accept her, once he knew the truth. It was enough to keep her silent for the entire journey, until Casper veered off the road to a slightly worn looking house and unlocked the door.

"Alright," he said, once they were inside. "What's going on?"

Alexia shoved her hands into her pockets, and then took them out again. Her heart was pounding so fiercely she could not speak. Then, just as she had worked up the courage to tell him who she was, two other figures ran into the room.

Alexia recognised them at once. Both had grown significantly since she had last seen them, but there was no mistaking little David's stick-out ears, or the joyful grin on Timmy's face as he clapped Casper on the back.

"You got out?" Timmy said. "I knew you would!"

"You had more faith than me, then," Casper said. "You all alright?"

David nodded. "We took care of the business for you while you were gone," he said. "He had clearly grown more talkative in the years Alexia had been away. "Didn't disappoint any customers. Business slowed a little, but we worked twice as hard, so it's all still here for you. The house and the carts and Ed the mule and all our customers too."

A relieved grin filled Casper's face. "That's great," he said. He didn't say it, but Alexia could tell that he had been worried. A spell in jail could mean disaster for any businessman, no matter how innocent he might be, but Casper could rely on his boys.

"How'd you get out?" Timmy asked.

"She admitted she was lying," Casper said. "All thanks to this fellow here." He nodded respectfully towards Alexia. "I don't know how I can repay you, sir."

"You can repay me," Alexia said, feeling suddenly bold, "by marrying me."

He looked at her in confusion. "What?"

"I'm Alexia, you dolt. Alexia Winters."

Casper stared at her for a long moment. She could see his eyes flitting up and down, taking in the details of her face, mapping it to that of the younger girl he once knew. "Alex?" he said.

"I'm surprised you didn't recognise me," she said. "But I did manage to convince you I was a boy for *years*. You're not the most observant."

"Alex!" Casper shouted, and he lunged forward and pulled her into an embrace. She wrapped her arms around him and squeezed him back, while the younger boys gaped at her in shock.

"You said Alex died!" said Timmy.

"I nearly did," Alexia said. "I ran from the fire at the workhouse and was struck by a carriage. I lost my memory for years. But once I remembered who I was and who *you* all were, I had to come back to you."

Casper released his hold on her and stepped back half a foot so he could look at her face again. "But that nun," he said. "She said you were at the convent."

Alexia grinned. "That was me," she said. She reached under her shirt and pulled out the locket that Casper had given her. "It'd been so long, and I didn't know you thought I was dead. I needed to know what you felt about me. So, I pretended to be a nun to talk to you."

"You should have told me," Casper said, pulling her into another embrace. "When I heard you were alive, Alex--"

"I know," Alexia said. "I was there, remember?" She laughed from sheer joy. "I knew I would find you again."

Casper stepped back, and the two other boys ran in to embrace her as well. Alexia smiled to be reunited with her family, but her gaze was still fixed on Casper. "You haven't answered my request," she said, after a moment. "Are you going to repay me for my help?"

"Yes," Casper replied, laughing. He grabbed her hand and pulled her away from the other two. "Marry me, Alexia. I've wanted no one else but you. You're the smartest, funniest, bravest, most resourceful person I know, and after thinking you were dead for so long, I am never letting you go again. Please be my wife."

"Hmm," Alexia said, tilting her head and smiling. "I'll consider it." Then she leaned forward and pressed a kiss to his lips.

Behind her, David made gagging noises in protest, and she tried to step back, still smiling, but Casper refused to let her go. He pulled her back in for another kiss, and Alexia obliged him, her heart singing.

Alexia and Casper were married in a small local chapel in Norwich, with the rest of the boys as witnesses. Alexia even bought a clean new dress for the occasion, and resolved never to steal other people's laundry again, unless it was really, truly necessary. Casper was overjoyed by Alexia's miraculous return to his life, and he could often be found watching his wife when he thought no one was looking, awe clear on his face. With her quick tongue and even quicker wit, they managed to expand the business even further, and they were soon known throughout Norwich as the couple to go to if you were a boy, or girl, who wanted an honest way off the streets.

Rebecca, for her part in events, was arrested for perjury and fraud, but Casper decided not to press charges against her. She had come close to ruining his life, but she had also indirectly helped him to reconnect with Alexia, and he felt some pity for her, as she was trapped in a hopeless situation. The damage that her actions and lies had done to her reputation was more than punishment enough. She was rarely seen at the butcher's shop after that, and later Alexia heard that she had left Norwich entirely to stay with family in another county.

John, the clerk, meanwhile, was fired from his position at the court for his role in the conspiracy, and although he did not face near the level of condemnation and gossip that Rebecca had to weather, he was known from that moment on as a dishonest sort of man, and he struggled to find either job or wife in the years to follow.

After years of struggle and tragedy, Alexia and Casper found joy with one another and with their eventual children, both born and adopted, and they lived happily ever after.

Thank you so much for reading. We hope you really enjoyed the story. Please consider leaving a positive review on Amazon if you did.

WOULD YOU LIKE FREE BOOKS EVERY WEEK FROM PUREREAD?

Click Here and sign up to receive PureRead updates so we can send them to you each and every week.

Much love, and thanks again,

Your Friends at PureRead

Printed in Great Britain
by Amazon